A Purnell book
ISBN 0 361 03853 4
First published 1977. Reprinted 1987
Copyright © 1977 Express Newspapers plc
Printed by Purnell Book Production Ltd
Paulton, Bristol. A member of BPCC plc
Macdonald & Co (Publishers) Ltd
Greater London House, Hampstead Road
London NW1 7QX. A BPCC plc company

RUPERT
and the Muddled Magic

Illustrated by John Harrold
Based on an original story by Frederick Chaplain

Purnell

CHAPTER 1

Rupert was walking through Nutwood village one bright sunny day when he saw his little friend Gregory Guineapig waiting at the bus stop. Gregory was holding his hand out to request the bus to stop.

"Good morning, Gregory," said the conductor cheerfully. "Where would you like to go today?"

But Gregory showed no signs of boarding the bus.

"I wonder what he's up to," muttered Rupert, mystified.

"Oh, I don't want to get on the bus," Gregory explained to the conductor. "I'm busspotting, and I just want to take the number of your bus. Look, here's my notebook and pencil."

The conductor frowned and became angry.

"Well," he said sternly, "that's too bad. The very idea! How dare you waste my time! These request stops are for people who want to travel on buses. I'm surprised you haven't more sense."

He rang the bell crossly and the bus moved off with a lurch.

Rupert had overheard and turned to his pal. "Hello, Gregory," he greeted him. "No wonder the conductor was so angry. You can't stop the bus just to take its number!"

Gregory looked upset. "Oh dear," he said. "Anyway, I was getting very bored bus-spotting. There aren't enough buses coming

by to make it interesting. I think I shall go train-spotting instead. Would you like to come too, Rupert?"

The little bear thought that was a very good idea.

"Let's go to Nutwood Halt," he suggested. "That's the nearest station.

But whatever you do, don't delay the trains as well."

Gregory agreed with a nod and a smile, and setting off together, the two pals soon reached the station.

"Wait a moment, Gregory," cried Rupert, as they neared the entrance. "I must go into the newsagent's shop for a notepad and pencil."

"All right," replied the little guineapig. "I'll go on ahead and meet you in the ticket office."

Gregory disappeared round the corner, and Rupert walked into the newsagent's shop. He peered all around the shelves until he found what he wanted.

"I'm going train-spotting," he told the man behind the counter. "That's why I need this notebook and pencil."

The man smiled. "What a good idea," he said. "But you'd better hurry. There's a train due in about five minutes."

"Oh, thank you," gasped Rupert, and handing the man the correct amount of money, he raced out of the door towards the station.

As he ran into the ticket office, Rupert could see Gregory waiting for him.

"Hurry up, Rupert," shouted Gregory. "I can hear the train coming now!"

"But we need to buy platform tickets," Rupert reminded him. "I've got my money ready. Have you?"

But the little guineapig took a long time to find his money, and then fumbled with the ticket machine.

"Oh, do hurry," cried Rupert. "I think the train is almost ready to leave again!"

Sure enough, as the chums ran on to the platform, they saw the end carriage of the train disappearing in the distance.

"Oh dear," said Gregory. "I'm very sorry, Rupert."

"Never mind," said his little friend. "They'll be another train soon. Let's ask the station master when it is due."

But when they found the station master he told them that they would have to wait two hours until the next train came in.

"That's a very long time," Rupert murmured. "What shall we do?"

Just then they saw the Chinese Conjurer walking down the platform.

"Hullo," the little chums greeted him. "What are you doing here? Are you going on a journey?"

"I was waving to my daughter,  Tigerlily," he explained. "She has gone to spend a holiday with her Auntie Ming, and now I have no one to help with my magic. I don't know what I shall do."

Gregory was very pleased to hear this. "Can I help you while Tigerlily is away?" he begged. "I can't spot a train for at least two hours, and I'm getting very bored."

The Conjurer looked doubtful. "I need a person who knows about magic to help me," he said. "Do you know about spells?"

Gregory had a sudden idea. "Oh yes," he cried. "Watch me, and I will show you a conjuring trick. Please help me, Rupert."

The little bear was rather hesitant. "I've never really done any magic before," he said doubtfully.

"Never mind," said Gregory. "I will show you what to do. Please give me your platform ticket."

Rupert did as he was asked, and then Gregory produced a large blue handkerchief from his pocket.

"Please tear our tickets into tiny pieces," he instructed the little bear, "and put them all into this hanky."

Rupert did so, wondering what his chum was going to do next, and when all the pieces had been dropped into the handkerchief Gregory tied the ends together. Then, closing his eyes, he muttered some odd-sounding words.

"What are you saying?" whispered Rupert.

"These are the magic words, of course," replied Gregory, rather crossly.

After a few moments the little guineapig opened his eyes. "Now watch carefully," he said.

He untied the ends of the handkerchief and shook it. As he did so all the pieces of the tickets fluttered to the ground.

"Oh dear," said Gregory unhappily. "I don't

think the magic has worked. The tickets should have become whole again."

The Conjurer was laughing. "It was a good try, little guineapig. I will take you as my assistant for a trial period."

"Oh, thank you," said Gregory happily. "That will be much more fun than train-spotting. Goodbye, Rupert."

Rupert waved to the Conjurer and Gregory as they walked off in the direction of the Conjurer's house.

"What shall I do now?" wondered the little bear. "I've got no one to play with and no platform ticket."

Rupert decided to abandon the idea of train-spotting. "I think I will try to find some of my other pals," he thought.

Leaving the station, Rupert discovered the postman standing by his van with a worried expression on his face.

"What's the matter?" asked the little bear.

14

15

"My van has broken down, and I've got an urgent parcel to deliver to the Squire," explained the postman.

"Don't worry," said Rupert. "I've got nothing to do. I will take the parcel to the Squire for you."

"That's very kind, little bear," said the postman, with relief. "But the Squire wants it taken to the castle ruins on the heath, and not to his home."

Rupert was puzzled, but still wanted to help. "Then I'll take the parcel there," he cried. "I'll go straight away."

"Thank you very much," said the postman, handing Rupert a large brown parcel.

16

CHAPTER 2

The little bear set off towards the heath carefully carrying the parcel.

"I wonder what it can be?" he muttered. "And why should the Squire be at the castle ruins?"

At length Rupert caught sight of the ruins in the distance.

"It's a very gloomy place," he said. "I hope I find the Squire soon."

Rupert began searching for him. He looked and looked but could see no one.

"I can't hear the Squire walking about," he said. "Perhaps if I call he will hear me. Is anyone there? Can you hear me? It's Rupert. I've got a parcel for you."

The little bear stood listening intently. Then he heard a muffled voice.

"I'm in the vaults. There are some steps that lead here. Come on down."

As Rupert gazed around he caught sight of a half-open door in the corner of the ruined room in which he was standing. He pushed the door wide open and peered down. Stretching down below him in the darkness was a flight of steep steps.

When Rupert reached the bottom the Squire was waiting for him.

"Hullo there," he said to the little visitor. "I was expecting the postman."

Rupert explained that the postman's van had broken down and that he had offered to deliver the parcel himself.

"That's very kind of you," said the Squire gratefully. "The parcel contains a lamp to help me see my way more clearly around the vaults. This torch isn't very powerful."

Then the Squire pointed to a yellow scroll of paper lying on the stone floor.

"Look at this, Rupert," he said. "When I

bought the land on which the castle ruins
stand I found this old scroll under some fallen
lumps of masonry. It's an old plan of the
castle, and there appears to be a secret room
in the vaults. But there doesn't seem to be any
way into it. I thought I could try to find it,
and that's why I need the lamp."

The little bear felt very excited as he gazed
at the map.

"Maybe I could help you search for the
secret room," he suggested, and he explained
how Gregory had gone with the Conjurer to
help with his magic and had left him alone.

"Very well," smiled the Squire. "You've
been so kind delivering the lamp, you shall
help me search."

Unwrapping the parcel and switching on the powerful new lamp, the Squire led the way through the dark passages. He paused in one of them and consulted the map again.

"I think the secret room should be in this area," he said. "But I've already looked and found nothing."

Just then Rupert fell headlong on the floor.

"Goodness me," he cried, feeling rather shocked, and brushing the dust off his clothes. I've just tripped over something."

The Squire knelt down and inspected the spot where the little bear had fallen.

"Look, Rupert," he said. "There's an iron ring in one of the flagstones. That's what you tripped over. Let's try to move it."

Together, Rupert and the Squire heaved at the ring. Suddenly the flagstone lifted up. The little bear peered underneath it.

"There's a key here!" he cried in amazement. "But it's very rusty. It must have been here for a very long time."

"Goodness me," said the Squire, holding up their find. "Do you suppose that this could be the key to the secret room?"

Meanwhile, Rupert was staring intently at the place where they had found the key.

"Come here quickly," he suddenly cried. "We didn't look carefully enough. There's a keyhole here in the floor. What an odd place to put one!"

The Squire bent down beside the little bear. "Let's see if the key fits," he said excitedly.

So Rupert's friend pushed the rusty key into the keyhole. It was very hard to turn.

"It's no wonder that

it's stiff," whispered Rupert to the Squire. "It can't have been used for a very long time."

Just then the key moved in the keyhole, and they heard a rumbling sound. To their astonishment, an opening appeared in one of the walls.

"Just look here, Rupert," shouted the Squire. "The key has made those two walls swing back. We must have found the entrance to the secret room!"

The Squire and the little bear crept gingerly through the opening in the walls. The Squire shone his powerful lamp all around. Amid the cobwebs hanging all round the room were strange bottles and vats.

Turning to Rupert, the Squire said, "So that's why the room has been kept secret for so long. It must have been used by a magician hundreds of years ago. Look, some of the bottles have still got liquid in them. And there's the fireplace where he would have heated his potions."

The Squire moved around the room, examining each object by the light of the lamp. Meanwhile, Rupert had discovered a piece of chain hanging above the fireplace.

CHAPTER 3

"I wonder what the magician used this for," Rupert thought, and he took hold of the chain and gave it a short pull. Suddenly the room filled with clouds of dust, and some bricks above Rupert's head crashed to the floor.

The Squire was alarmed. "Quickly, Rupert, you've dislodged that brickwork. We must get out of the room before we are trapped."

The Squire and the little bear ran quickly through the opening in the walls. Shining the lamp ahead of them, they retraced their steps to the flight of stairs.

"Hurry to the top as fast as you can," shouted the Squire urgently.

When they reached ground level again they sat on some rocks to recover.

"That was a close shave," said the Squire, mopping his brow. "I was afraid that the roof was weak and would collapse on top of us."

Then Rupert had an idea.

"Let's go up to the battlements," he suggested. "We can get some fresh air there and recover from our shock."

They climbed to the battlements and looked out over the heath. Rupert could see the Conjurer's house in the distance.

"Look," he cried, "that's where Gregory has gone to help the Conjurer."

As he gazed at the house the little bear noticed something curious.

"That's odd," he muttered. "The Conjurer's house seems to be swaying!"

Rupert pointed the house out to the Squire.

"I expect it's just a trick of the light," the Squire said. "Maybe the heat haze is making the walls look as if they're moving."

On their way home the Squire told Rupert that in the morning he intended to prop up the weak roof in the secret room.

"Maybe you could ask your mother if you could help me," he suggested.

"That would be nice," replied the little bear. "I would like that. Now I'm going to see Gregory in the Conjurer's house on my way home."

Bidding goodbye to the Squire, Rupert trotted towards the Conjurer's house. As he drew near, he noticed all sorts of objects flying out of the windows of the house. Rupert was astonished. "Whatever is happening?" he thought.

Entering the house, Rupert found the Conjurer looking very agitated.

"My magic went wrong," he explained. "First

I tried to make little Gregory vanish, and now I can't find him. And now objects in my house are all flying about out of my control."

"So that's why all those things were flying out of your windows," said Rupert.

The Conjurer nodded sadly. "Some strange power is making my magic useless," he sighed. "If I don't find out what it is I cannot bring your friend back."

Rupert was very alarmed. "But you *must* find Gregory," he pleaded. "He must be here somewhere."

The little bear began to look all around the room. Just then he heard a strange sound.

"What's that noise?" he cried. "It came from over there," and he pointed to a large stone jar standing in the corner. He peered over the edge of the jar, and at the bottom he could just see the little guineapig, squeaking faintly.

"Thank goodness you've found me, Rupert," said Gregory breathlessly. "I didn't think the trick was ever going to finish. It's so dark and lonely in this jar. Please pull me out."

Rupert helped his little friend clamber out of the jar, and then the pals returned to the Conjurer. He was sitting in his chair looking very dejected.

"Thank you for finding him, Rupert," he said. "But I don't understand what happened. The magic should have put him in the cabinet, not the jar. Why didn't it work?"

Just then the Conjurer had an idea. "Perhaps Gregory isn't suited for magic," he suggested. "Come here, and we'll find out."

He led the chums towards an odd-looking machine in the next room. Gregory was feeling rather upset.

"It's not my fault," he whispered to Rupert. "I only did as I was told."

"Come over here," ordered the Conjurer.

He stood the two little pals next to the machine, and asked them to hold two knobs.

"Watch the dials," he said. "They tell if one person is better for magic than another."

"They both show the same reading," cried Rupert. "So you see, it wasn't Gregory's fault that the magic went wrong!"

"That's not enough proof," answered the Conjurer. "We must have other tests."

CHAPTER 4

The Conjurer led Rupert towards a curtained cabinet. "Please go in," he said. "I will try a vanishing trick with you."

The little bear looked anxious, but did as he was told. The Conjurer closed the curtains and began to speak strange words in a soft, monotonous voice. At length Rupert began to feel dizzy, and then he felt himself being spun round and round.

"Oh dear," he gasped, "What's happening to me?"

When the little bear recovered he found himself sitting on a large metal ring which hung from the ceiling of a high room. Sitting beside him Rupert saw a parrot.

"What do you think you're doing?" the parrot squawked angrily. "How dare you land on my perch!"

Rupert explained to the parrot what had happened, and gazed around the unfamiliar room.

"I think I am still in the Conjurer's house," he murmured. "I must try to find my way back to the others."

Still feeling a little dizzy, Rupert made his way along all sorts of passages until at last he heard Gregory's voice in a nearby room.

"Your magic has gone wrong again," the little guineapig was squealing. "What have you done with my chum?" Rupert ran into the room and explained his adventure, and how he had landed on the parrot's metal ring.

"I'm very sorry," the Conjurer apologised,

"but something is spoiling my magic. Maybe I can find it in this book of spells."

The little pals decided that it was time to go home. "My Mummy will be very worried about me by now," said Rupert.

Gregory told the Conjurer that he would come and see him again tomorrow. "Perhaps you will have solved the mystery by then," he said rather anxiously.

Mr and Mrs Bear were much relieved when Rupert reached home, and after having tea, the little bear explained his extraordinary adventures.

"The castle ruins don't sound very safe," said Mrs Bear with a worried expression.

"Don't worry, Mummy," cried Rupert. "I shall be very careful when I go back tomorrow."

When Rupert woke up the next morning he saw a little figure walking past his house.

"Why, it's Gregory on his way to help the

Conjurer," he said. "Hullo, Gregory!"

The little guineapig looked quite downcast. "Hullo, Rupert," he muttered. "I'm not very keen on being the Conjurer's assistant again. It's not much fun when the magic doesn't work."

"Don't worry," chuckled Rupert. "Maybe the Conjurer has found out what's wrong with his magic by now."

With a sigh Gregory shuffled on his way to the Conjurer's house. Later, after breakfast, the little bear said goodbye to his mother.

"Now, do be careful at the castle," she warned, "and make sure you stay close to the Squire."

"I'll be careful, Mummy," promised Rupert, as he bounded out of the door.

When Rupert arrived at the castle ruins he found the Squire already hard at work.

"Hullo, little bear," he smiled. "I've been working since the sun came up, and I've already managed to prop up some of the roof in the secret room. Perhaps you could stay here and sort out some more timber for me while I continue working downstairs."

Rupert agreed and set to work. He was sorting the timber into various sizes when he spotted a dark shape in the sky across the heath.

"I wonder what that could be," he thought. "I shall be able to see it when it gets closer."

As the shape drew nearer the little bear cried out in amazement. "It's Gregory!" he shouted. "He's flying through the air!"

"Help me, Rupert!" squealed his little pal, as he sailed over Rupert's head. "One of the Conjurer's tricks has gone wrong again, and I've become light and I'm floating away!"

Rupert had a sudden idea. Running up to the battlements, he reached over the side as far as he could without falling off. He managed to catch hold of the little guineapig's sleeve and pull him on to the battlements.

"You're safe now," he said.

At length his little chum recovered. "I feel much heavier now," Gregory said. "Thank you very much for helping me, Rupert. I won't ever go and help the Conjurer again."

As they looked down over the battlements Gregory suddenly squeaked in fright.

"Oh, goodness me! There's the Conjurer walking towards the castle. Do you think he's come to find me? I won't go back there. I won't!"

CHAPTER 5

Rupert persuaded Gregory to meet the Conjurer.

"I'm sure he's come to see that you're safe," he said. "We had better see what he wants."

The two pals climbed down the steps and found the Conjurer waiting for them.

"I'm pleased you're safe, little guineapig," he said. "Sorry my magic didn't work again. But I discovered something as I came to find you." He pointed to his magic wand.

"Look," he said, "it trembles. It trembled as soon as I started to walk towards the castle. There must be other magic coming from here. Now I shall follow the wand and see what I find."

The Conjurer held the wand in front of him, and walked forward, guided by the quivering object. The two chums followed nervously.

"Look," whispered Rupert, "He's walking down the steps to the vaults."

Turning round, the Conjurer said, "The magic is powerful here. Look at the wand!"

The Conjurer followed the passage along, guided by the light from his wand. It trembled more and more until at last the little party found themselves outside the entrance to the secret room.

"This is the room the Squire and I found yesterday," cried Rupert in excitement. "Look, the wand's leading us into it!"

As the little group entered the room the Squire, who had been at work there mending the fallen brickwork, came over and greeted them. After they had explained how the wand had led them there, the Squire said, "We discovered that this room was once used by a magician. Is that why the wand is trembling?"

The Conjurer was already gazing around the room. "A magician certainly lived here once," he

said, "and he cast many powerful spells. Now I know why *my* magic won't work."

The friends stared at him in astonishment. "What do you mean?" asked the Squire.

"Many spells were locked up in this room," explained the Conjurer. "When you opened the door you let them out. They are more powerful than my magic and so they spoil it."

"But what can we do?" Gregory asked unhappily.

"I must break the old spells," the Conjurer replied. "then my magic will be strong again. You must leave the room and let me work."

The Squire and the two little pals agreed to do so.

Hurrying towards the door, they stepped outside and then stood peeping round the doorway so that they could watch the Conjurer at work.

First of all he fetched several bottles covered in cobwebs from the shelves. Putting liquid from each of

these into a large bowl, he began stirring the
mixture with his wand. As he did so, smoke
rose from the bowl, and the Conjurer began
chanting strange-sounding words.

"What's he saying?" whispered Gregory.

"I can't hear very well," replied Rupert.
"You must be quiet, or you'll disturb the
charm he's making. Just look at all the smoke
that's coming from the mixture now!"

As Rupert finished speaking the room was
suddenly lit up with a glow from the bowl. It
cast eerie shadows all over the room and the
two little pals were very frightened.

"Don't worry," the Squire comforted them.
"He knows what he's doing."

At length the glow died away, and the
Conjurer waved his wand over the bowl
again. There was a sudden flash of light
which dazzled the little group watching
from the doorway, and then bright stars

rained down all over the secret room.

Gregory was trembling from head to foot. "Now what's happening?" he said shakily.

'I think the Conjurer has finished his charm," whispered Rupert. "The stars are almost gone now."

At length the Conjurer walked over to the little group.

"My charm has broken the old spells," he smiled. "My magic will work again now. Look, my wand isn't trembling any more!"

"But how can you be certain that the old spells have been broken?" asked Rupert rather nervously.

"We can test it with a very simple trick," said the Conjurer, laughing. "Come over here and help me."

CHAPTER 6

"Hold this plate," said the Conjurer to the little bear.

Then he gave the Squire a match, and handed the little guineapig a candle.

"Stand between them, Rupert," the Conjurer commanded, "and shield the candle with the plate. Squire, please light the match."

The Squire did so, and after the match was lit, the Conjurer raised his wand. Just as the match went out the Conjurer waved the wand and the candle lit up.

"Well," cried the little bear. "However did you do that? The plate was between the match and the candle!"

"That proves my magic is all right now," laughed the Conjurer.

"Hooray!" cried Rupert. "You really have broken the old spells!"

The Conjurer asked the Squire if he could explore the secret room more fully.

"Of course," beamed the Squire. "While you are looking round I will show Rupert and Gregory the work I have done on the roof."

Leading the little chums towards the fireplace, the Squire pointed upwards. "That was where the bricks fell away yesterday when you gave the chain a tug, Rupert," he smiled. "As you can see, I've put some of the timber on the roof to support it. It's quite safe now."

"Does that mean I could bring my chums here to see what we've discovered? Would you show them the secret room and the way it opens?"

"Of course," smiled the Squire.

At that moment the Conjurer aproached. "Excuse me," he said excitedly. He was

holding a dusty green bottle with a long thin neck, containing some dark brown liquid.

"This liquid is very special," explained the Conjurer. "It contains very rare magic that I have been seeking for many years."

"Then you must have it," said the Squire kindly.

Bowing low to the Squire and the two pals, the Conjurer made his way out through the doorway. As he walked away the little guineapig began to follow him.

"Where are you going, Gregory?" cried Rupert. "You said you would never help the Conjurer again."

"That was when his magic was being spoilt, and I kept vanishing or floating in the air," explained Gregory. "But now his magic is working again, and it will be much more fun being his assistant!"

Rupert and the Squire waved goodbye to the little guineapig.

"What an extraordinary day we've had, little bear," said the Squire. "I didn't expect the ruined castle to hold so many secrets. And now I've got one more surprise. Follow me."

They were soon out in the open air again.

"Are you hungry, Rupert?" inquired the Squire.

"Oh yes!" Rupert cried.

The Squire laughed. "I thought that we might get hungry when you came to help me this morning, so I packed a large hamper."

As the little bear and the Squire sat munching their food, Rupert chuckled. "I never imagined that train-spotting could lead to so many adventures!" he said.